Emma Thomson's

felicity Wishes

Little book of

Every Day Wishes

h

Hodder
Children's
Books

A division of Hodder Headline Limited

January

Happy New Year!

⭐ 1st

Stay happy and really believe in your
dreams this year.

⭐ 2nd

Take a deep breath and make a sparkling wish
for a brand new year.

⭐ 3rd

Wish for fun and happiness the whole year through.

☆ 4th

Wake up from your dreams
with a smile, and your wishes may come true.

☆ 5th

Snuggle up by the fire and make a warm,
winter wish.

☆ 6th

Make a quick wish in 30 seconds... Starting now!

☆ 7th

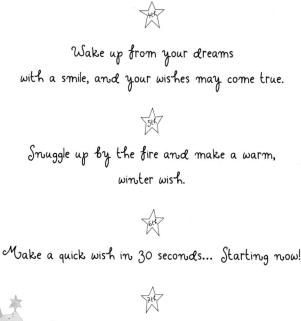

Point your nose in the direction of
your dreams, and wish!

☆8th☆

Make a wish first thing in the morning
and last thing at night. Double wishes!

☆9th☆

On a rainy day, wish for sunshine
and warmth.

☆10th☆

Close your eyes, quietly listen to your dreams,
and make a wish.

☆11th☆

In a dizzy moment, make a silly, giddy wish!

☆ 12th ☆

Hold hands with your best friend and say your
wishes together at the same time.

☆ 13th ☆

Make a wish when you see a bird
and it may just come true.

☆ 14th ☆

Dance all your winter blues
away with a sunny, happy wish!

☆ 15th ☆

On a perfect day, make a perfect wish.

16th

Believe in your dreams and your wishes
may come true.

17th

Make a wish that makes you feel warm
from your nose to your toes!

18th

Close your eyes, stretch out your arms,
and make a huge wish.

19th

Look for the blue in the sky and make a wish.

When the wind blows, run in its direction
and make a wish.

Stand on your tiptoes and make a
wish for something scrummy.

On an ordinary day, make an
extraordinary wish!

This is the day for surprises.
Make a wish you never dreamed would come true!

Delicious!

Grant yourself a super, fantastic,
great hair day!

Catch a raindrop on the tip of your
tongue, count to ten and make a wish!

You look so good!

Concentrate hard, wrinkle your forehead
and make a wish.

Stand still for a moment and think about
today's wish. What will it be?

4th

Skip to the top of a hill and sing your wish
to the world.

5th

Make a wish as you walk with your
hands in your pockets.

6th

If you sneeze three times, make a wish on
the third sneeze!

7th

Try to make your wishes
come true by really believing in your dreams.

☆ 8th

When things are looking grey and cloudy...
wish for sunshine and blue skies.

☆ 9th

Treat yourself to an extra special wish today.
What will it be?

☆ 10th

Grant yourself a day of chocolate naughtiness!

☆ 11th

Stand out and make a wish that is a little bit different!

☆ 12th

Make a wish on a moonlit sky... for the happiest dreams tonight!

☆ 13th

Giant sushi!

As you write your Valentine's card, make an extra special wish for your Valentine.

☆ 14th

Wear something red and wish for love –
it's Valentine's day!

My heart's all a-flutter!

☆ 15th

Believe in your dreams and they may just come true.

☆ 16th

When you see a bird, stand on your tiptoes...
and make a wish!

★ 17th

Surprise yourself and make a dazzling wish
when you least expect to.

★ 18th

Make a wish for a super, smiley day.

★ 19th

Turn your daydreams into real dreams
by making a wish!

★ 20th

Make a special wish for someone close
to your heart.

⭐ 21st

When the phone rings, make a quick
wish before you answer it!

⭐ 22nd

Make a wish as soon as you open your sleepy
eyes in the morning.

⭐ 23rd

Find somewhere quiet and make a secret
wish just for you!

⭐ 24th

Tap your toes, smile and make a special wish.

☆ *25th*

On a starry night, pick out the brightest star in the sky and make a wish!

☆ *26th*

If you need a friend, make a wish for them to be there.

☆ *27th*

Make a happy wish for a happy day!

magic
fairy
wings

☆ *28th*

Make a wish to be a fairy for the day!

☆ *29th*

If it's a leap year, make a leaping wish!

March

⭐ 1st

It's springtime.
Make a wish on a butterfly.

⭐ 2nd

Spread a little happiness and make a wish
for each of your friends.

⭐ 3rd

Grant yourself a day of lots of yummy things!

☆ 4th

Make a wish to follow your dreams and
who knows what could happen!

☆ 5th

Make a wish just before you close your
eyes at night. Goodnight!

☆ 6th

Stop and think about today's wish.
What will you wish for?

☆ 7th

Blink three times, spin round
and make a wish.

☆ 8th

Wish for a day where the fairies do all your work!

☆ 9th

Plant a seed, make a wish and
watch it grow!

☆ 10th

Get up early and make a wish before
the sun rises.

☆ 11th

Make a brave wish for something
you never dared to wish for before.

☆ 12th

Spring-clean your wish list and
make a fresh, new wish.

☆ 13th

When you least expect it, make a wish!

☆ 14th

Whisper today's wish three times
and it may come true.

☆ 15th

Make a wish when you cut a
slice of yummy chocolate cake.

⭐ 16th

Add a little sparkle to your life...
Make a dazzling wish!

⭐ 17th

Make a special wish and send it to
your favourite person!

⭐ 18th

Remember to keep today's
wish a secret. Shhhh!

⭐ 19th

Chocolate brownies, lime jelly and strawberry cake.
Wish for them all!

☆ 20th

Make a happy wish as soon as you wake
up in the morning.

☆ 21st

Make a silly, sunny,
funny, upside-down wish.

☆ 22nd

Wink at the moon and
make a glowing wish.

☆ 23rd

Make a wish on the
first spring flower you see.

Things look good from here!

24th

Grant yourself a day of fun, fun, fun! Enjoy!

25th

Spin round and round, and make a dizzy
wish on your third turn.

26th

As the first snowdrops appear,
make a gentle wish.

27th

Make a sunny wish even when it rains!

28th

Five, four, three, two, one... Wish!

29th

Wish on a star and watch the night stars twinkle to make it come true.

30th

A little piece of magic may just come true if you make a wish today.

31st

Make a big wish and don't miss anything out!

I hope your wish comes true!

April

★ *1st*

One perfect white cloud in a blue sky...
means one perfect wish might come true!

★ *2nd*

Take three deep breaths and wish
all your worries away.

★ *3rd*

Make a wish for everyone you know.

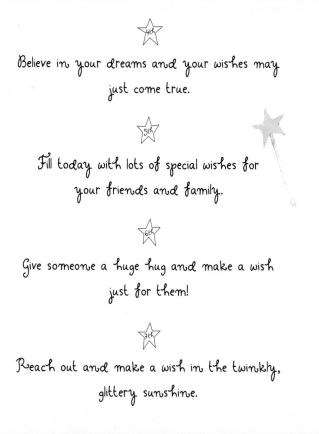

4th

Believe in your dreams and your wishes may just come true.

5th

Fill today with lots of special wishes for your friends and family.

6th

Give someone a huge hug and make a wish just for them!

7th

Reach out and make a wish in the twinkly, glittery sunshine.

Make a wish to be filled with peace
from your nose to your toes.

Take a walk in the sunshine or in the rain...
and make a wish.

Reach for the stars and make
your dreams come true.

Eeny, meeny, miny mo.
What will you wish for today?

Grant yourself a wishy-washy hour
in a relaxing bubble bath.

When things seem a little mixed-up,
make a wish to unscramble them!

Wish for all the things you love,
and then some more!

Don't tell anyone your secret today...
or it might not come true!

16th

Close your eyes, lie back and think
hard before you make today's wish.

ADMIT
ONE
FAIRY

17th

Make this the day for
lots of fun wishes!

18th

Walk through the woods and
make a wish on a beautiful flower.

19th

When the moon smiles at you,
smile back and make a wish!

☆ 20th

Wish for happy days when you are
down in the dumps.

☆ 21st

Spin round three times one way and then
three times the other way. Wish!

☆ 22nd

Write down today's wish and
remember to keep it secret!

☆ 23rd

Throw a daisy into the wind
and make a wish as you let go.

This wish is for you!

Take a giant step and make a huge wish.

Make a wish for something special...
and it might just come true!

Make a wish with a best friend over a frothy,
creamy milkshake.

Be your own person and make
a special wish just for you!

☆ 28th

Wish on a star and let
your dreams shine brightly.

☆ 29th

Jump up and down three
times, spin round and
round twice and wish!

You can do it!

☆ 30th

Really believe in your dreams and your
wishes may come true.

May

☆ 1st
Whisper today's wish so
no one can hear.

☆ 2nd
Close your eyes tight and wish hard.
For your wish may just come true!

☆ 3rd
Wishes come true when you least
expect them to... Make a wish!

☆ *4th*

Sing a silly, funny wish to yourself.
Enjoy!

☆ *5th*

Throw a coin into water
and make a wish!

ONE PENNY

☆ *6th*

Blue skies, green fields, yellow buttercups –
wish on something beautiful.

☆ *7th*

Wish on a bird carrying a
flower in its beak.

8th

Make a wish on a white cloud and
it may just come true!

9th

Help your wishes come true by
following the path they lead.

10th

Stand on your head and
make a topsy-turvy wish!

11th

As the clock chimes twelve,
make a striking wish!

☆ 12th

When you see a shooting star, make a twinkly wish.

☆ 13th

Treat yourself and make a yummy wish that's good enough to eat!

☆ 14th

Repeat today's wish three times and it may just come true.

Irresistible!

☆ 15th

Smile as soon as you wake up, and make a happy wish.

16th

Make a wish on the most beautiful flower
for a blossoming day.

17th

Click your heels together three times
and make a wish.

18th

Make a wish for someone who is
always there for you. They deserve it!

19th

Look in the mirror and
make a wish just for you!

☆ *20th*

If you want your dreams to come true,
you have to make a wish!

☆ *21st*

Tie a piece of cotton around your little finger
and make a wish.

☆ *22nd*

Hold something you love close to
your heart, and make a wish.

☆ *23rd*

Visit a friend — and make
a friendship wish together.

24th

Spend five minutes thinking about
a special wish for today.

25th

Hop on one leg, do five star jumps and
make an energetic wish!

26th

Fairy cakes, chocolate brownies and apple turnovers –
wish for lots of yummy things!

27th

Make a wish on the first beautiful
thing you see in the morning.

☆ 28th

Oops! Don't forget to
make a wish today!

☆ 29th

Dream larger, wish harder and
your wishes may just come true.

many wishes so little time!

☆ 30th

Make a big wish for the world.

☆ 31st

Cross your fingers and toes for good luck
and then make a wish.

Summer

June

⭐ 1st

Wherever you go or whatever you do,
make a wish to brighten up your day.

⭐ 2nd

On a special day make an extra
special wish for happiness.

⭐ 3rd

Red, yellow, pink and green – make a rainbow wish!

4th

Take all the time in the world
to make today's wish...

5th

Close your eyes and visit the place
where dreams come true. Wish!

6th

Spread a little sparkle and make
wishes for all of your friends.

7th

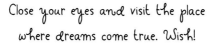

Make a wish for your most
fabulous dream to come true.

☆ 8th

When things are a little dull,
make a silly funny wish!

☆ 9th

Take a giant leap and make a giant wish!

☆ 10th

Hold hands with your best friend
and make a friendship wish!

☆ 11th

Spoil yourself and make a naughty
wish for yummy things!

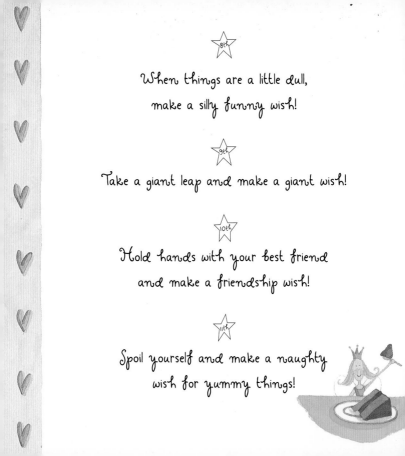

☆ 12th

When you have butterflies in your belly
and your legs have turned to jelly, make a wish.

☆ 13th

Make a wish on all the beautiful
things around you.

☆ 14th

Wish for fun and laughter,
and enjoy the rest of the day.

☆ 15th

Sniff the petals of a pretty pink rose
and make a wish.

☆ 16th

Make a tiny wish with a whisper for
something big and loud!

☆ 17th

Make a wish from the tips of your fingers
to the bottom of your toes.

☆ 18th

Stand on one leg, hop three times
and make a silly wish!

☆ 19th

Take a break and make
today's wish.

☆ *20th*

When things look a little scary, wish for
all your troubles to go away.

☆ *21st*

When you see a flower in full bloom,
make a blossoming wish.

☆ *22nd*

Make a wish and who knows
what will come true!

☆ *23rd*

Balloons, streamers and cake — make a party wish!

24th

Take a walk in the sunshine and smile
when you make today's wish.

25th

Pick the brightest flower you can find...
and make a wish!

26th

Wish for something you've always wanted,
and it might just come true!

27th

Make the ordinary extraordinary
with just one wish!

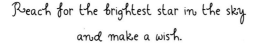

Reach for the brightest star in the sky
and make a wish.

Make a wish when
you open the front
door for a wonderful day.

A tiny wish is just as
powerful as a big wish!

I wonder what it will be?

July

☆ 1st

Whenever you need a friend,
close your eyes and make a wish.

☆ 2nd

Eeny, meeny, miny mo!
What shall you wish for today?

☆ 3rd

An ice-cold drink, suntan lotion and an ice cream –
make a summer wish!

☆ 4th

Make a wish and repeat it five times to yourself.
It may just come true!

☆ 5th

Wish for a bit of fairy magic
to come your way.

☆ 6th

Make a wish and follow it
wherever it may lead.

Map

☆ 7th

If you see a butterfly on a summer's day,
make a wish as it flutters by.

⭐ *8th*

Sit amongst the flowers and the trees,
and make a beautiful wish.

⭐ *9th*

There are lots of yummy things in life –
wish for them all!

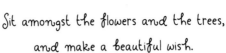

⭐ *10th*

When you need a lift, make a sunny wish to
brighten up your day.

⭐ *11th*

Make a wish for perfect picnic weather.

☆ 12th

Catch up with a friend and make a wish
over a scrummy, frothy milkshake.

☆ 13th

Make an extra special wish for someone
close to your heart.

☆ 14th

Make a wish for all your favourite things...
just not at the same time!

☆ 15th

As you lick the drops off your ice lolly,
make a summery wish.

16th

Jump up and down three times,
turn around twice and make a wish!

17th

Sit back, relax and wish away!

18th

Lie in the warm summer grass and whisper
your wish to yourself.

19th

Wish for goodies and they may come true!

I'm busy wishing!

20th

Don't get distracted — let the phone ring and make your wish in peace.

21st

Wish for two of your favourite things in one wish!

22nd

As you watch the sun go down, make a wish for another great day.

23rd

Make a silly, sunny, funny wish!

✩ 24th

Make a wish for a bit of magic
to come your way.

✩ 25th

Make a wish for all your favourite chocolate treats.

✩ 26th

Put on your brightest dress and
make a colourful, sparkly wish!

✩ 27th

Swap your favourite wish with your
best friend and see what happens.

28th

When you least expect to,
surprise yourself and make a fantastic wish!

29th

Make a special wish for
something you need.

30th

Take a walk in the sunshine and make a
sunny, happy wish.

31st

Grant yourself a day
of being lazy!

August

☆ 1st

One, two, three, four... Wish!

☆ 2nd

Close your eyes and whisper your wish to yourself.

☆ 3rd

Send a text wish to your fairy godmother.
It may just come true!

☆ 4th

Whenever you need a friend,
close your eyes and make a wish.

☆ 5th

Grant yourself a day of special treats.

☆ 6th

Place the tip of your first finger on your nose
and make a secret wish.

☆ 7th

Sometimes wishes you don't mean
to make might just come true!

On a cloudy day,
make a wish for sunshine.

☆ 9th

Everyone's different so be yourself
and make a wish especially for you!

☆ 10th

Make a wish and remember
to keep it safe and secret.

☆ 11th

Make a daisy chain and say
a wish every time you add a flower.

☆ 12th

Make a wish come true by
really believing it can happen.

☆ 13th

Close your eyes in the warm summer sun
and make a wish.

☆ 14th

Wish for your favourite treat.
It may just come true!

☆ 15th

Before you wish, stop and think about what you've
always dreamed of. Now wish!

Bake a fairy cake and wish all
your worries away.

Make an extra special wish for you
and your best friend.

Stand tall on your toes, and wish for happiness!

Make a wish each time you see a bird and
let magic flutter into your heart.

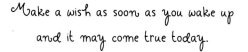

Make a wish as soon as you wake up
and it may come true today.

It's summertime! Wish on the brightest flower
in your garden.

Make a wish for your favourite
dream to come true!

Get up early and make a happy wish
before the sun rises.

24th

Clap your hands together three times
and make a wish.

25th

Make a dazzling wish on a bright, sunny day.

26th

Take a walk in the countryside
and tell a rabbit your wish.

27th

Look high into the summer sky
and wish on a distant cloud.

Red, yellow, green and blue –
make a colourful wish!

Grant yourself a day of special treats. Yummy!

Make a wish and then another one!
Two wishes today!

When you're feeling a little blue,
wish on something sunny.

Autumn

September

☆ *1st*

Make a wish every day and, one day,
your wishes may come true.

☆ *2nd*

Sit under an apple tree, catch a
falling apple and make a wish.

☆ *3rd*

Make a wish for a dream to come true.

4th

Dance around your garden
three times and make a wish.

5th

Treat yourself to an extra special wish today.
What will it be?

6th

Count backwards from ten and when you reach
number one, whisper your wish.

7th

Write your wish down. Keep it in a
safe place and, one day, your wish
might come true.

8th

Make yourself smile with a wish
for your dreams to come true.

9th

Bake a dreamy chocolate cake and
make a wish on the first gooey bite.

10th

Reach for the stars and make a dazzling wish.

11th

Wriggle your nose, think of a number
under ten and make a wish!

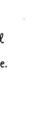

Make a wish for someone
close to your heart.

Let the phone ring and quickly
make a wish before you answer it.

Make a wish to forget about
your worries for one day.

Take ten deep breaths and
slowly make today's wish!

16th

Wish on the stars for a dazzling day ahead.

17th

Even a little wish can go a long way,
so don't forget to make your wish today.

18th

Big, small, tiny – make a wish whatever the size!

19th

Make a wish for lots of
yummy, scrummy things.

⭐ *20th*

Make a special, sparkly wish for your friends.

⭐ *21st*

Jump up and down three times and
make a wish in mid-air!

⭐ *22nd*

Lie on top of a hill, close your eyes tight
and make today's wish.

⭐ *23rd*

Sparkly make-up and magic hair
mousse – make a pampering wish!

☆ 24th

Decisions, decisions.

What will you wish for today?

☆ 25th

When you see your reflection in a puddle:
wish for something special.

☆ 26th

Make a magical wish for a magical day.

☆ 27th

When you're walking down the street,
make an everyday wish!

Spend time with friends and family
and wish for lots of fun and smiles.

Make a sunny wish on a rainy day
and let it brighten up your day!

Spoil yourself and make a wish
just for you!

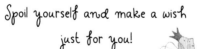

Bliss!

October

1st

Bake fairy cakes and make a wish when
you take the first bite!

2nd

Walk through a puddle and make a
big splash as you wish.

3rd

Treat yourself to a scrummy, yummy wish!

☆ 4th

Make a warm wish in a hot, steamy bath.

☆ 5th

Share a wish with your friend and
make it come true together.

☆ 6th

Conkers, golden leaves and crisp mornings –
make an autumn wish.

☆ 7th

Curl up and read a good book.
Make a wish as you turn
the last page.

☆ 8th

When you are a little lonely,
make a wish for someone to be there.

☆ 9th

Make your dreams come true
with a special fairy wish.

☆ 10th

Hold on to your dreams and
remember to make your wish today.

☆ 11th

Whisper your wish through your letter box!

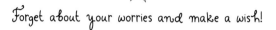

Face mask, conditioner and lots
of bubbles — treat yourself!

Forget about your worries and make a wish!

Make a wish to shop until you drop!

Celebrate friendship and make a
wish with your best friends.

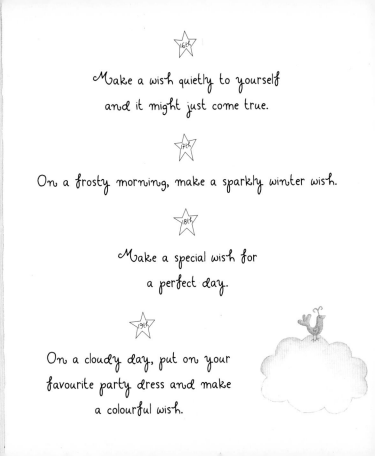

⭐ 16th

Make a wish quietly to yourself
and it might just come true.

⭐ 17th

On a frosty morning, make a sparkly winter wish.

⭐ 18th

Make a special wish for
a perfect day.

⭐ 19th

On a cloudy day, put on your
favourite party dress and make
a colourful wish.

☆ *20th*

Put your hand on your heart and
make a special wish for someone you care about.

☆ *21st*

Make all your wishes come true by really
believing in yourself.

☆ *22nd*

It's autumn!
Make a wish on a golden leaf.

☆ *23rd*

Hot chocolate, log fires, cosy blankets –
wish for lots of warm things.

Stick your tongue out to catch a raindrop
and make a wish.

When things are a little grey,
make yourself a silly wish.

Hug someone dear to you and make a warm wish.

Catch a falling leaf and make an autumn wish.

28th

Grant yourself a super, fantastic wish!

29th

Close your eyes, sink into a bubble bath
and make your wish for today.

30th

Join hands with your friends
and make a friendship wish to last forever.

31st

Make a wish for a special Hallowe'en treat.

November

⭐ *1st*

Make a warm wintry wish – just for you!

⭐ *2nd*

Wish on the brightest star in the sky and the night
stars might just shine for you.

⭐ *3rd*

Snuggle down in your favourite chair and really
think about today's wish.

☆ 4th

Wish on a falling snowflake, or a raindrop!

☆ 5th

Bonfires, fireworks, sparklers –
make a glittering, colourful wish.

☆ 6th

Make a wish for someone who
is always on your mind.

☆ 7th

Grant yourself a day of pampering!

8th

On a crispy, cold morning,
whisper your wish to a robin.

9th

On the first bite of scrummy
chocolate cake, make a wish.

☆ 10th

Make a warm wish for someone
close to your heart.

☆ 11th

Send sparkly wishes to
your family and friends.

⭐ 12th

Wrap up warm and go on a long wintry
walk to think about today's wish.

⭐ 13th

Put on your party dress, do a little
dance and make a party wish!

⭐ 14th

If you need a shoulder to cry on,
make a wish for a friend to be there.

⭐ 15th

Have fun today and make
a topsy-turvy wish!

I'm here!

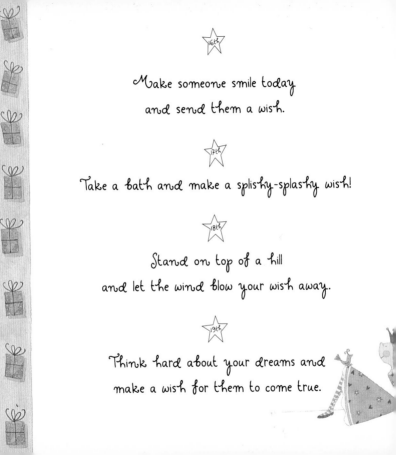

☆ 16th

Make someone smile today
and send them a wish.

☆ 17th

Take a bath and make a splishy-splashy wish!

☆ 18th

Stand on top of a hill
and let the wind blow your wish away.

☆ 19th

Think hard about your dreams and
make a wish for them to come true.

⭐ 20th

Blink three times and make a special fairy wish.

⭐ 21st

Lie on your back, point your toes to the sky,
and make a wish!

⭐ 22nd

Wish on something beautiful for a beautiful
wish to come true.

⭐ 23rd

Cold nights, dark days –
wrap up warm and make a bright wish!

☆ 24th

In a dizzy moment,
make an upside-down wish.

☆ 25th

When you see the first snowflake of the year,
make a special wish!

☆ 26th

Wish on something beautiful and
your wish may just come true.

☆ 27th

Shower yourself with wishes today.
You deserve it!

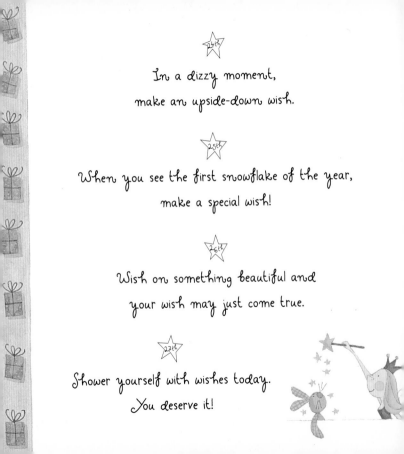

☆ 28th

Cold mornings, icy paths and frosty trees –
make a wish on a wintry day.

☆ 29th

Forget about your worries and
make a new wish for a new day.

☆ 30th

Dance by the light of the moon
and wish for happy times.

December

1st

Log fires and fairy sing-songs –
make a warm, wintry wish.

2nd

Write your wishes in a letter to Santa
and who knows what will come true!

3rd

When you see a robin, stand on your tiptoes
and make a wish on its red breast.

☆ 4th

As the snowflakes fall, make a sprinkling of wishes.

☆ 5th

When you make a Christmas cake,
stir the mixture with love and make a wish.

☆ 6th

Curl up in a chair and make a warm
wish from your toes to your nose.

☆ 7th

Let's party! Wish for an exciting day.

☆ 8th

Mince pies, Christmas pudding and sweeties –
wish for lots of yummy things!

☆ 9th

When you see a snowman, make a wish.

☆ 10th

Decorate your house and
make a tinselly Christmas wish.

☆ 11th

Make a wish for those far away
from you at this special time of year.

Fall over in the snow and make
a wish that no one sees!

Be generous and make a wish
for the whole wide world!

As you write your Christmas cards,
make an extra special wish for your friends.

When you put the first bauble
on the Christmas tree, make a wish.

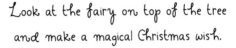

As you wrap your presents for the ones
you love, wrap a Christmas wish too.

Look at the fairy on top of the tree
and make a magical Christmas wish.

18th

Put on your party outfit
and make a sparkly wish.

It's snowing!
Make a winter wonderland wish...

Make a wish, wrap it in a snowball
and throw it as far as you can.

Treat yourself this Christmas
and make an extra special wish!

Build a snowman, add eyes
and a nose, and make a wish!

Christmas is coming... Make a
wish for something special.

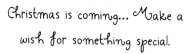

I wish I had a scarf like yours!

★24th★

Hang up your stocking, close your eyes
and make a wish. Who knows what you will get?

★25th★

It's Christmas! Believe in the magic of
Christmas and let your wishes come true.

★26th★

Pull a Christmas cracker with someone
special and make a wish just for them.

Merry Christmas!

★27th★

Christmas is for making all your wishes come true.
Make a wish!

28th

Make a special wish on the brightest star in the sky.

29th

Catch a snowflake in your hand,
and make a wish before it disappears.

30th

Sprinkle wishes around your bedroom
for a dazzling day.

31st

As the clock strikes twelve,
make a magical wish for the New Year.

With this book comes a
special everyday wish:

Hold the book in your hands and
close your eyes tight.
Count backwards from ten and
when you reach number one, whisper
your wish...
...but make sure no one can hear.
Keep this book in a safe place and,
maybe, one day, your wish will come true.

Love
felicity
x